This book belongs to:

这本图画书属于：

_____

_____

_____

The
BIGGEST BADDEST
WOLF 坏坏狼

〔英〕尼克·沃尔德 文·图　思　铭 译

"I am the GREATEST!"
"我是最最伟大的"！

howled Harum Scarum, admiring himself in the mirror as he brushed his fangs. "I am the biggest, baddest, hairiest, scariest wolf in the city!"

坏坏狼欣赏着镜子里面正在刷牙的自己，嚎叫起来。

"我是城里最强壮、最邪恶、毛最浓、最可怕的狼！"

Harum Scarum looked at his watch.

"Time for some fun," he said.

坏坏狼看了看表说：

"是该去找点儿乐子的时候了。"

Harum Scarum's idea of fun was to scare people. Well, he was the biggest, baddest, hairiest, scariest wolf in the city!

"Have I got everything?" he wondered, patting his pockets.

"Money, sweets, Teddy ... Oops, where's my teddy?"

Nobody knew that Harum Scarum had a teddy, and that he couldn't go anywhere without him.

坏坏狼找乐子其实就是去吓唬人。谁叫他是城里最强壮、最邪恶、毛最浓、最可怕的狼呢！

他拍拍口袋，检查一下，"该带的都带了吧？"

"零钱、糖果、泰迪……哎哟哟，我的泰迪熊呢？"

这是个小秘密，没有人知道坏坏狼一刻也离不开他的泰迪熊，没有它坏坏狼哪儿也不去。

'Ah! There you are!" he sighed, giving Teddy a big, wet, wolfy kiss.

"啊！我可找到你了！"他长舒了一口气，给了泰迪一个湿乎乎的狼式亲吻。

He put Teddy in his back pocket and went off happily.

他把泰迪熊放在裤子后面的口袋里，高高兴兴地出门去了。

First stop was the park where Harum Scarum had some fun scaring all the little children playing on the swings.

吓唬人的第一站是公园，坏坏狼喜欢吓唬那些正在荡秋千的孩子们，他觉得很过瘾。

"Run, little children, run,
or I'll eat you up!" he howled.

"快逃啊，小孩儿，快逃，
不然我马上就把你们吃掉！" 坏坏狼大声吼道。

"Eeek!" they screamed and rushed away.

"哎呀！" 孩子们尖叫着。

"I am the biggest, baddest, hairiest, scariest wolf
in the city!" he called after them.

"我是城里最强壮、最邪恶、毛最浓、最可怕的狼！" 他在后面喊着。

Harum Scarum moved on to the bus stop where a group of old people were waiting.

坏坏狼又来到公共汽车站，这里有许多老人正在等汽车。

"Run, old people, run, or I'll eat you up!" he howled.

"快逃啊，老家伙，快逃，
不然我马上就把你们吃掉！" 坏坏狼大声吼道。

"**Eeek!**" they screamed, and tottered all the way home.
"I am the biggest, baddest, hairiest, scariest
wolf in the city!" he called after them.

"哎呀！" 老人们吓得大叫，摇摇晃晃地逃回家去了。
"我是城里最强壮、最邪恶、毛最浓、最可怕的狼！"他在后面喊着。

For the rest of the day Harum Scarum worked very hard at scaring anyone he could.

在这一天剩下的时间里，坏坏狼使劲地吓唬他遇见的每一个人。

He **startled** a skateboarder ...

他把一个玩儿滑板的男孩子吓坏了……

He **petrified** a builder ...

他把一个建筑工人吓呆了……

And he made a street juggler jump.
"This is fantastic fun," he cried.

他把一个街头艺人吓得跳了起来。

"这真是太好玩儿了！" 坏坏狼高兴地说。

By the time he got home, he was so tired he decided to go straight to bed.
And that's when he discovered ... he'd lost his teddy!

坏坏狼回到家的时候已经累坏了，于是他决定马上睡觉。

这时候，他忽然发现……他的泰迪熊不见啦！

"Oh no!" he said, frantically searching his room. He looked here and there ...but he couldn't find Teddy anywhere.

"天啊，不会吧！" 他开始慌慌张张地把屋子翻了个底儿朝天。

这儿找找，那儿找找……可就是找不到他的小泰迪！

Harum Scarum crawled sadly into bed.
He tossed and turned, but he couldn't get
to sleep without his teddy to cuddle.

坏坏狼难过地爬上床。

没有泰迪熊，他翻来覆去地怎么也睡不着。

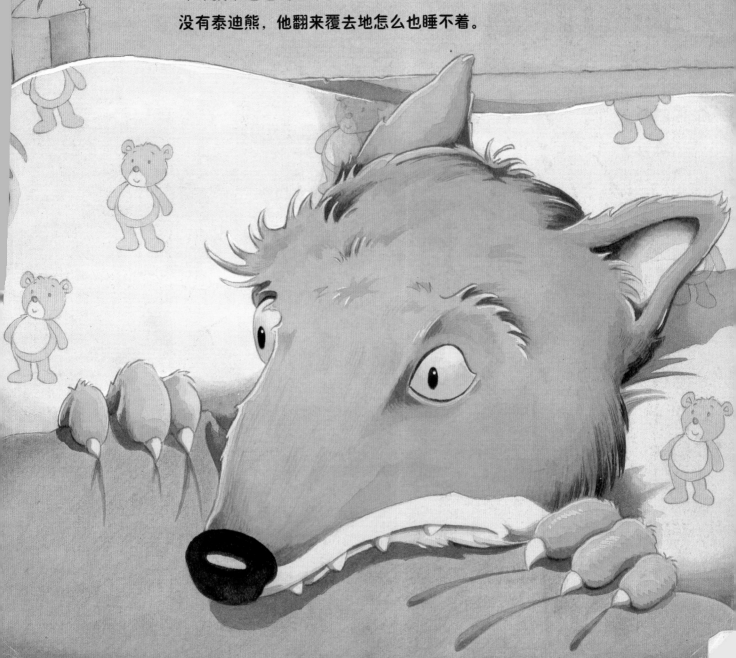

The next morning Harum Scarum was a nervous wreck.
"I must find my teddy," he wailed, and hurried outside
without even brushing his fangs.

第二天一大早，坏坏狼简直是没精打采。

"我必须找回我的泰迪。"他哭哭啼啼的，连牙也顾不上刷就匆匆忙忙地出门了。

He paced the streets.

他在街上走来走去。

He searched in every alleyway.

每一条小巷他都找遍了。

He looked high ...
他爬到楼顶上找啊……

Teddy!
泰迪啊！

and low...

又爬到地底下找啊……

Teddy!
泰迪啊！

But Teddy was nowhere to be seen.
可是泰迪还是不见踪影。

Finally he arrived at the bus stop.
"Excuse me, have you seen a teddy?"
he asked the old people.

最后，他来到了公共汽车站。
"不好意思，你们看到我的泰迪了吗？"
他向那些老人们问道。

But as soon as they saw him they tottered
off home shouting, "Help, it's the biggest,
baddest, hairiest, scariest wolf in the city!"

可是老人们一看到坏坏狼，吓得马上逃回家去啦，边跑边喊：
"救命啊！城里最强壮、最邪恶、毛最浓、最可怕的狼来啦！"

Harum Scarum went to the park.

"Excuse me..." he began, but the little children all rushed off shouting, "Help, it's the biggest, baddest, hairiest, scariest wolf in the city!"

坏坏狼又来到公园里。

"不好意思……"他才刚开了个头儿，可是孩子们马上就四处跑开啦，他们喊着：

"救命啊！城里最强壮、最邪恶、毛最浓、最可怕的狼来啦！"

Harum Scarum sighed, and a tear rolled down his cheek. But just then he noticed one little boy left playing on his own. And he was playing with ...Harum Scarum's teddy!

坏坏狼叹了口气，几滴眼泪流了下来。就在这个时候，他看见一个小男孩儿一个人留在草地上玩儿。他正在玩儿——坏坏狼的泰迪！

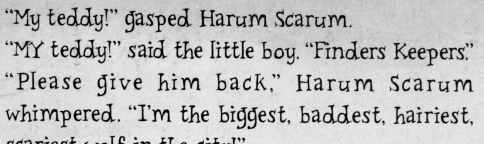

"My teddy!" gasped Harum Scarum.
"MY teddy!" said the little boy. "Finders Keepers."
"Please give him back," Harum Scarum whimpered. "I'm the biggest, baddest, hairiest, scariest wolf in the city!"

　　"我的泰迪！"坏坏狼猛地吸了一口气。

　　"我的泰迪！"小男孩儿说。"谁找到算谁的！"

　　"求求你把它还给我吧，"坏坏狼小声央求说。"我是城里最强壮、最邪恶、毛最浓、最可怕的狼！"

"You don't look so scary to me," said the little boy.
"Please!" cried Harum Scarum. "I'd do anything to get Teddy back."
"Do you promise to do exactly what you're told from now on?" smiled the little boy.
"Of course," he said.

"我一点儿也不怕你！" 小男孩儿说。

"求求你！" 坏坏狼都快哭啦。"只要你把泰迪还给我，我愿意做任何事！"

"那你能保证从今以后都听我的，按我说的做吗？" 小男孩儿笑着问。

"当然啦！" 坏坏狼回答说。

The very next morning, after a good night's sleep, Harum Scarum brushed his fangs and patted his pockets.

Whistling happily, he left home and went straight to the park.

"Hurry up" cried the little children.

"We're on the swings! Come and push us."

"Coming," smiled Harum Scarum. He trotted up to the children ...

紧接着第二天早晨，美美地睡了一觉的坏坏狼满意地刷着他的大牙，拍拍他的口袋。

他愉快地吹着口哨走出家门，径直向公园走去了。

"快点儿！"孩子们大声喊他。

"我们在荡秋千，快来帮忙推一下！"

"来啦！"坏坏狼笑着说。他一路小跑地来到孩子们那边……

"Eeek!" cried the children, rushing off.
"You promised..."

"哎呀！" 孩子们尖叫着，向四处逃去。

"你不是保证过……"

"Well, what did you expect?" chuckled Harum Scarum, hugging his teddy.
"You should NEVER trust the biggest, baddest, hairiest, scariest wolf in the city!"

"嘿嘿，你想什么呢？"坏坏狼得意地笑着，抱着他的泰迪熊。
"你们永远也不要相信城里最强壮、最邪恶、毛最浓、最可怕的狼！"